Unicorn Magic

Sweetblossom
and the New Baby

Daisy Meadows

Special thanks to
Karen Ball
For Rumi – the very sweetest
new blossom

ORCHARD BOOKS

First published in Great Britain in 2021 by The Watts Publishing Group

1 3 5 7 9 10 8 6 4 2

Text copyright © 2021 Working Partners Limited
Illustrations © Orchard Books 2021
Series created by Working Partners Limited

A CIP catalogue record for this book is available from the British Library.

ISBN 978 1 40836 145 0

Printed and bound in Great Britain by Clays Ltd, Elcograf S.p.A.

The paper and board used in this book are made from wood from responsible sources.

Orchard Books
An imprint of Hachette Children's Group
Part of The Watts Publishing Group Limited
Carmelite House
50 Victoria Embankment
London EC4Y 0DZ

An Hachette UK Company
www.hachette.co.uk
www.hachettechildrens.co.uk

Unicorn Magic

Sweetblossom and the New Baby

Daisy Meadows

ORCHARD

Contents

Story One
Dawn Days

Story Two
Midday Mayhem

Story Three
Spring Baby Sunset

Meet the Characters

Aisha and Emily are best friends from Spellford Village. Aisha loves sports, whilst Emily's favourite thing is science. But what both girls enjoy more than anything is visiting Enchanted Valley and helping their unicorn friends, who live there.

Sweetblossom

Sweetblossom is the unicorn in charge of spring in Enchanted Valley, bringing warmth, sunny days and new babies to the magical land. Her special lockets help to make the season perfect for everyone to enjoy.

Fluffy little Philip the featherhog is especially excited that spring is nearly here, because he's looking forward to becoming a big brother!

Philip

Queen Aurora

Queen Aurora rules over Enchanted Valley and is in charge of friendship; there's nothing more important than her friends. She has a silver crown, and a beautiful coat which can change colour.

Selena is a wicked unicorn who will do anything to rule over Enchanted Valley. She'll even steal the magical lockets if she has to. She won't give them back until the unicorns crown her queen.

Selena

Spellford

Enchanted Valley

An Enchanted Valley lies a twinkle away,
Where beautiful unicorns live, laugh and play.
You can visit the mermaids, or go for a ride,
So much fun to be had, but dangers can hide!

Your friends need your help – this is how you know:
A keyring lights up with a magical glow.
Whirled off like a dream, you won't want to leave.
Friendship forever, when you truly believe.

Story One

Dawn Days

Chapter One
A Sunrise Surprise

Aisha and Emily peeked out of the flap of their tent into the dark night. They wore the new onesies that they'd found laid out last night on their sleeping bags as a holiday surprise. Both onesies were covered in a unicorn print. Aisha's had a silver unicorn horn dangling from her hood. Emily's had a gold horn.

They'd arrived at Daffodil Dunes Campsite yesterday afternoon for a weekend away with Emily's parents. It was their first time camping and it had been such fun to sleep in a tiny tent all by themselves. They'd chattered long into the night over a midnight feast of chocolate chip cookies.

This morning's special treat was an exciting one. The four of them had agreed to wake up early to see the sun rise! Outside it was dark right now, but they knew that soon the sun would peek over the horizon. The sky would turn into a blaze of colour and all the birds would start singing! Emily's dad had brought his bird-spotting book especially, to take notes.

"Come on, girls!" Emily's dad said, emerging from his tent next door. "It's nearly time."

Emily and Aisha had never seen a sunrise before – not here, anyway! Of course, in Enchanted Valley they'd often seen the sparkling sun rising over a magical world. That was a kingdom that only the two best friends knew about –

a place full of unicorns and mermaids, dragons and all sorts of magical creatures.

The two of them scrambled out of their tent. By the light from her phone's torch, Emily's mum started pouring hot chocolate into mugs.

But just as they were about to join the adults, Emily noticed something out of the corner of her eye – two glowing dots that shone from the pockets of their onesies. Emily shared a glance with Aisha.

"Brrrr!" Emily called to her parents. "We're just going back for a blanket."

Inside the tent again, they pulled out the keyrings from their pockets. The keyrings had been given to them by their unicorn friend, Aurora. She was the queen of Enchanted Valley. Aurora used the keyrings to call on the girls when the creatures of the valley needed help.

"I hope it's not that awful Selena," Aisha whispered. Selena was a bad unicorn, determined to steal Queen Aurora's power and rule Enchanted Valley for herself. The girls knew she would turn it into a horrible place to live.

Emily peeked back out of the tent where her mum and dad had settled down to

watch the sun rise. "They'll never notice we've gone," she said. Time didn't pass in the human world when they were in Enchanted Valley – even on holiday!

The two girls clutched their keyrings and brought the unicorn horns together. In an instant, they were surrounded by a glittery cloud of sparkles. The ground

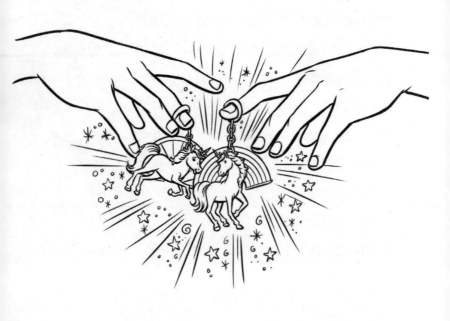

disappeared from beneath their feet as they floated up into the air. Their bodies felt as light as feathers! Then they drifted down and felt their feet come to rest on grass.

As the sparkles faded, they saw they were on a slope of lawn beside Aurora's beautiful, golden palace. The dawn sun glowed weakly above its twisting turrets, which looked like unicorn horns.

Before the palace stood Queen Aurora, smiling down at them. Her coat was all the different colours of the sunrise – just like the one they'd been about to see back home! Pink and orange, red and purple. Around her neck she wore the powerful Friendship locket. Beside her stood a small creature, its eyes crinkled in a toothy grin. It looked rather like a

groundhog – almost like a large squirrel – but covered in feathers instead of fur, and with a fluffy tail.

The friends went to greet Aurora, putting their arms around her.

"We're so happy to see you again!" cried Emily.

"How can we help?" asked Aisha, pulling back. She was sure they were here to do something important. "Is it Selena again?"

"No." Queen Aurora shook her head, her mane sparkling. "I brought you here to introduce you to Philip – he's a featherhog."

Philip cleared his throat and lifted the tip of his chin into the air, his downy feathers wavering in the breeze. He began to talk in a loud, careful voice as though addressing a huge crowd. "You're here for a very special reason. Very special indeed."

He seemed so grand that Emily wondered if she and Aisha should drop into a curtsey! Then Philip's face split into a grin and the next thing they knew, he was hopping from foot to foot, punching the air with every word that

came next. "You're here for our Spring Beginnings Festival!" He stopped his dance, paws still raised in the air, his eyes shining. "That is, if you'd like to come?"

The two friends shared a glance, their faces flushed with delight. Philip wasn't grand at all. He was just excited – and so were they!

"Yes, please!" Aisha and Emily cried.

Chapter Two
A New Friend

Queen Aurora's delicate hooves left a trail of prints in the frost. The girls ran to catch up with her, their breath sending out smoky clouds.

"I like your outfits," Aurora said, with a smile, as the girls showed her the unicorn horns on their hoods.

"They're lovely and warm too," said Emily.

"That's good," said Aurora. "I know it's cold at the moment, but that's where Philip will help us. It's his job to wake up Sweetblossom."

Aisha frowned. "I don't understand. Why would that make the weather warmer?"

The queen gave a beautiful smile. "Sweetblossom is the unicorn in charge of starting springtime," she explained.

"And once that's begun," piped up Philip, "the festival can begin, too. You'll see!" He hopped along beside Aurora, his long, feathery tail streaming out behind him.

"Where are we going?' asked Aisha.

"To Dapplelight Wood," Philip said.

"That's where Sweetblossom hibernates."
He puffed his chest out proudly. "My
family is in charge of waking her each
year, and this year it's my turn! My mum
and dad say I'm old enough now. It's a
great honour, you know!"

"I'm sure it
is," said Emily,
winking at
Aisha. Philip
was taking
his job *very*
seriously.

Philip
clapped his
paws together.
"Spring
Beginnings is a
very important

day. It's the day when all the spring babies will be born."

"And?" Aurora prompted him, her eyes twinkling beneath her long eyelashes.

"And I am going to have a baby brother!" Philip cried. He suddenly stopped in his tracks, and Aisha and Emily nearly stumbled into him.

"What is it?" Aisha asked, looking around. "Is something wrong?"

"I just realised," Philip said. "I haven't got my new brother a present." His little brow creased in a frown, his feathery eyebrows sinking over his eyes. "I'm the worst brother in the world." He flumped on to the ground, his head drooping so low that his nose disappeared amongst the feathers of his little round tummy.

"Oh no!" Emily knelt down beside him.

"I promise you're not."

"And we'll help you get him something," Aisha added, patting his head gently.

Philip looked at the girls hopefully. "What do you think I should get him?"

Aisha and Emily shared a glance, thinking.

"A rattle?" Aisha suggested.

"A blanket?" Emily said.

Philip shook his head. "He already has those things as family hand-me-downs. I want to give him something special and all his own." He wrapped his arms around himself and anxiously tugged at his feathers. "Oh, what could it be?"

The two girls came to put their arms around him until they were in a giant, feathery hug! They squeezed him tight until his feathers tickled their noses and made them burst out into laughter.

"We'll think of something!" Aisha said. "Don't worry."

Philip cheered up, looking around again and sniffing the air. "Tally ho!" He pointed a paw in the direction of some far distant trees and bounded ahead of them.

Emily and Aisha stood on the edge of Dapplelight Wood. The early-morning light cast the trees in a golden glow. Along with Queen Aurora and Philip, they stepped beneath the trees and listened to the birdsong as the dawn chorus began. It was as though the whole forest had woken up to welcome them.

"These birds' songs are very different to the ones back home!" Aisha exclaimed.

"I think that's because the birds are different," said Emily, as she gazed up into the treetops.

"That's a Star-ling!" Philip said, pointing. Sure enough, a small bird of purple and green flew through the air leaving a trail of glittering stars behind it. Emily wished she had her dad's bird-spotting notepad, so that she could draw a quick sketch.

"What's that one?" Aisha waved at a bird who was chirping out the strangest giggle.

"Can't you guess?" Philip asked. The girls shook their heads. "It's a Blue Tittering!"

The girls laughed as the Blue Tittering landed in a tree.

As the friends continued to pick their way through the forest, some of the birds flew down to follow them. Their feathers were every bright colour and their proud little tummies fluffed up as they darted through the air like a rainbow of carnival streamers behind the girls.

"Ever onwards!" Philip cried, hopping and skipping ahead of them.

The four of them walked in single file between the trees, but as they got deeper into the forest, they heard sounds behind them. There was the scuffling of leaves, and bubbling laughter.

Emily looked back and saw clusters of unicorns, phoenixes darting through the air, and even a little dragon hiccupping flames. They were all so cute! Minky the kitterfly swooped low over their heads and the girls called out hello. Pixies and gnomes crept out from behind rocks and

soon all the forest creatures had followed them into a clearing.

Aisha gasped. "The whole forest has come out to join us!"

"Yes," Queen Aurora said, "we all come to see this every year."

In the centre of the clearing was a circle of snowdrops. Dew clung to their tiny white heads and they sparkled like diamonds in the morning sun. Inside the circle slept a unicorn.

"That must be Sweetblossom!" Aisha whispered. The unicorn had a pale pink coat, like a spring flower in a meadow. Her mane and tail were the soft blue of a sunny sky, and her horn pressed against her flank as she curled up tightly. She let out gentle snores and Aisha laughed.

"I've never heard a *pretty* snore before,"

she said. "But why is she sleeping here?"

Emily frowned. "And where is her locket?" There was nothing round the unicorn's throat.

"Actually," Aurora said, coming to stand beside them, "Sweetblossom has three lockets. She takes them off when she sleeps through the winter."

Philip hopped over the tiny flowers, his feathers ruffling in the breeze.

"He'll wake up Sweetblossom now," Queen Aurora whispered into their ears.

Aisha and Emily waited for Philip to tap Sweetblossom's shoulder or gently call her name but instead he began to … dance! Their eyes grew wider and wider as they watched him jig, hop, pirouette and skip around the sleeping unicorn. His feathers rose up around his body into

an amazing fan that looked just like a miniature peacock's tail! All the time, he sang:

"Hop to the left
Give a shake.
It's time for our friend
Sweetblossom to wake!"

The two friends couldn't help laughing, but they quickly stopped when they noticed a stirring in the heart of the snowdrop circle.

"Look!" Aisha whispered. The two of them crept closer to watch as Sweetblossom's gentle snores stopped. Then her long eyelashes fluttered open. She was waking up! The unicorn got to her hooves and gave herself a good stretch as she yawned.

"Good morning!" she said, as though she'd only had a short nap. She looked surprised to see everyone. "Is it time for spring to begin?"

"YES!" everyone cried. "Good morning, Sweetblossom!"

"Now, watch," Queen Aurora whispered. "She'll go to those three crocuses for her lockets. That's where she keeps them when she hibernates."

"Ah, I see!" Emily looked around and, sure enough, there was a patch of purple crocuses peeping out of the grass. Apart from the snowdrops, they were the only flowers in the glade. Sweetblossom trotted over to them, and lowered her velvety nose to find her lockets.

But she gave a neigh of alarm.

Sweetblossom backed away from the flowers, trembling.

"What is it?" Queen Aurora called over.

Philip ran over to join Sweetblossom and peered at the crocuses. "Oh no!" he cried.

Sweetblossom turned to face them. "The lockets," she said, her voice breaking. "They've gone!"

Chapter Three
An Unwelcome Visitor

Instantly, a determined look passed over Philip's face and his feathers stiffened with resolve. "We have to find the lockets!" he cried. The little featherhog leapt about from bush to tree. He snuffled beneath piles of leaves and poked his nose into tufts of grass.

Emily and Aisha started to search too and then all the other creatures did the same. They raced around the forest, looking for the lockets.

"Do you think this could be Selena's work?" Emily whispered to Aisha. Selena was always trying to steal the unicorns' lockets in the hope of taking control of

Enchanted Valley.

"Maybe," Aisha said. "It would be just like her."

Aurora called over to the girls. They went to join the queen and Sweetblossom.

"Sweetblossom, this is Emily and Aisha." Aurora gave a warm smile. "They have been a great help to me."

Sweetblossom looked close to tears. "Emily, Aisha," she said in a shaky voice. "I've heard about you and all the problems you've solved in the valley."

"We could help again!" Emily said quickly.

"If you'd like us to," Aisha added.

Queen Aurora dipped her head. "I was hoping you'd say that."

"Yes please," said Sweetblossom, a tear finally escaping from her eyes. Emily put a comforting arm around her neck, whilst Aisha patted her mane.

"What do the lockets look like?" Aisha asked gently.

"There is the Longlight locket," Sweetblossom said. "It's in charge of making the days longer and looks like a shining sun. Then there's the Blossoming

Buds locket. That has a cherry blossom in the middle. Finally, there's the Bouncing Baby locket. That has a picture of a chick hatching."

There was a sudden flash of lightning and the girls threw their hands up to cover their eyes. When they dared to look again, a silver unicorn with a blue mane and tail stood beside them. A cry of despair rang around the forest from all the animals.

"Selena!" the girls cried.

"You did this, didn't you?" Queen Aurora said.

The evil unicorn laughed, throwing back her head so that her long, sharp horn slashed through the air. "Of course I did! And even if you find the lockets, you won't dare get them back. The days will stay short and cold for ever, no flowers will open, and none of the spring babies will be born … unless, of course, you make me queen of Enchanted Valley!"

"Never!" the girls yelled.

"Have it your way," Selena snarled. "But you'll be begging for the lockets by the end of the day, and then you'll *have* to make me queen!"

With another flash of lightning, she cackled and disappeared.

The gnomes and pixies gathered around as the kitterflies and dragons hovered above their heads. Everyone looked worried and a trembling kitterfly flew to Emily for comfort.

"What are we going to do?"

Sweetblossom whimpered.

"Don't worry, Sweetblossom," Aisha said. "Emily and I will find the lockets."

"We promise!" added Emily, joining her friend.

"You'll only have today to get them back," Queen Aurora reminded the girls. "If the sun goes down before we get the lockets back, the days will stay short, seeds won't grow and the spring babies won't be born."

"We don't have much time," said Philip. "The sun sets so early in winter!"

Emily and Aisha hadn't thought of that. But they could see the look of hope in Sweetblossom's face. Their new unicorn friend believed in them, and they wouldn't let her down.

"We need to think about this calmly,"

Emily said. "We should start at the very beginning." Emily loved science and she was always able to think about things in a practical way. "Can you show us the flowers where the lockets are usually kept?"

"Of course!" Sweetblossom trotted back over to the crocuses and the girls followed her.

The three of them gathered around

the little purple flowers, half-hidden in the grass. In the middle of the patch of crocuses were three broken stalks, bent and crushed into the mud.

"They're ruined," said Sweetblossom, her head drooping.

"But look!" Aisha pointed to a little pile of purple petals beside the crocuses. Near the pile was a row of even more petals.

"It looks to me as though someone left a trail," Emily said, her heartbeat growing faster in her chest. She shared a glance with Aisha, who was grinning.

"What are you going to do?" Sweetblossom asked.

Aisha and Emily gave each other a high five. "Follow it!" they cried.

Chapter Four
Forest Trail

The friends were about to set off but
Aurora hesitated. "I think I should go
and protect the palace," she said. "Selena
might try to take it. But will you be OK
without me?"

"Yes, you go back to the palace," Emily
said. "We'll find the lockets, don't worry."

Aurora touched her whiskery nose to their cheeks. "Thank you." Then she trotted off through the forest. The girls were all alone with Sweetblossom now … or *almost* alone.

"I'll come too, and help you follow the trail!" It was Philip, hopping from foot to foot, his feathers rippling. "I have a baby brother I want to meet today. Best foot forward!" he cried, scrabbling along the

row of purple petals that led beneath the trees.

Emily and Aisha ran to catch up with the little featherhog and Sweetblossom trotted behind. They were both glad to have two friends with them ... especially when the trail led them deeper into the forest. The winter light was pale and watery – it was like stepping into a dark maze. They had to watch where they put

their feet. The air grew cooler around them and they were glad to be wearing their onesies!

The trail of purple petals led them to a clearing.

"Where now?" asked Aisha, brushing a spider's web off her onesie.

Emily looked around, then pointed to a cave at the edge of the clearing. A sign stood beside it, painted in dripping white letters. The words were all wonky and covered in splodges, but the message was clear. It read:

Cranky's Cave
DO NOT DISTURB!

"Look," said Philip. "The petals lead right into the cave." He peered up at the

others, his face serious. "We have to go in."

"But who's Cranky?" Emily wondered aloud.

"And is he as cranky as his name?" Aisha asked.

From inside the cave there suddenly came a huge noise on a gust of wind that sent their hair flying back over

their shoulders. The friends ran behind a
rock. Then they peeked out, the tips of
their noses resting on top of it.

"What was that?" Emily whispered. Was
it the growl of a terrible monster coming
to life?

A second noise – just like the first

– came rumbling out of the cave on another gust of horrible, smelly air. There was a pause, and then another noise, just like the others.

Emily cocked her head on one side, listening. "I think … I think …" She got to her feet. "It's a giant snoring!"

"There's only one way to find out!" said Aisha, already heading around the rock.

The three of them tiptoed into the cave. It was even gloomier in there! But from the sunlight that streaked past them, they could just make out the outline of a gigantic figure lying in the dirt. Even asleep, it towered over them. It had thick, matted fur, and claws that glinted in the shadows. They could make out long, yellow teeth where the creature's mouth hung open. And that huge mouth belonged to an even bigger ... bear!

As they watched, the bear turned over on the cave floor and tucked his knees up to his big tummy. There was a patch of cave floor that was empty now and – there! The girls spotted something silver shining beneath the bear's bottom.

Sweetblossom's face lit up. "My lockets!"

"I can't believe we've found them already," Emily gasped. "We'll just need to wake up the bear and ask him for the lockets, won't we?"

"And we have Philip with us!" Aisha added, grinning. "If anyone can wake the bear, it's Philip!"

"Yes, he did an excellent job with me," Sweetblossom agreed.

Philip beamed with pride. "Happy to help." He bowed low.

"Although," Sweetblossom let out an anxious whinny, "maybe we shouldn't wake him. Bears can get very grumpy when they're woken up. Remember the sign outside."

"Sweetblossom's right," said Aisha, her face falling as she looked over at the bear. She shuddered as she saw the claws that glinted on one of his outstretched paws. "Remember, Selena said we wouldn't *dare* get the lockets back. I bet that's why she hid them here with him."

"Well, that's where she's wrong," Emily said, folding her arms. "We just need to think about this."

Aisha was still looking at the bear. In his sleep, he moved his paw to scratch his round belly. Beside the animal was another, smaller bear. It had fallen out from under his paw. This one wasn't snoring – it was a cuddly toy!

"I've never seen a bear with a teddy bear before." Emily giggled, despite the scary situation.

"How do we get the lockets back without waking him?" Philip asked.

But Aisha felt a flutter of hope. If this giant bear needed a cuddly toy to sleep, maybe he wasn't as scary as he looked. "I think we need to be brave," she said.

"Let's try giving him a nudge," Emily suggested. "We just need him to move a little so we can grab the lockets from under him."

They went over to the bear and looked for a good place to nudge him. Aisha went up towards the bear's head and leaned against his huge shoulder. Her hands disappeared into his thick brown fur, and she found it was surprisingly soft. She pushed her weight against him, worried that he might wake up …

… but nothing happened. And he didn't move.

Emily came and stood next to her and Aisha instantly felt a little less scared. Together, the two of them leaned all their weight against the bear and managed to rock him slightly. Not too much – just enough so that he'd shift over a bit.

Nothing.

All he did was snore even louder.

They straightened up. Philip had come to stand on the other side of them.

"Would a song help?" he said hopefully.

"You're good at waking creatures up," Aisha said, "but we're trying *not* to wake him!"

"Perhaps if you sing very softly." Emily held a finger to her lips.

Philip began to hop from foot to foot.

"*Bear, oh bear!*" he sang quietly.

"Sleeping there,
with your soft, soft fur,
we need you to stir."

The bear didn't move. Emily and Aisha exchanged a glance. How would they get the lockets if they couldn't make him move?

Chapter Five
A Tickle Too Far

Sweetblossom was watching from a safe distance. Gently, she called out a suggestion. "Tickle him!"

It was a good idea, but … "With what?" Emily whispered. They looked around at the cave's floor.

Philip's eyes lit up. He reached behind

him and with a *ping!* he pulled out one of his longest, most feathery feathers.

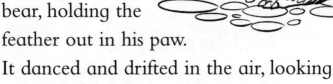

He started to approach the bear, holding the feather out in his paw. It danced and drifted in the air, looking more than a little tickly.

The girls walked down to the bear's bottom, where the lockets were trapped beneath his weight. They wanted to be ready to grab them when the bear moved.

"Ready?" Philip called softly, his voice trembling.

They each gave him two thumbs up.

Philip reached out with the quivering tip of the feather and drew it back and forth over the bear's nose. The bear's face twitched in his sleep and he gave a low grunt of annoyance. Then he … began … to … move!

The friends all shared a glance and Aisha crossed her fingers, hoping this would work. Otherwise, they were all about to become a bear's breakfast!

The enormous creature dragged a paw across his face, as though getting rid of an irritating insect. Then he shifted his haunches and moved a tiny bit across the cave floor.

"Quick!" Aisha said. She managed to snatch up one of the lockets, holding it up in the air like a prize. It was the Longlight locket, with its little sun glowing inside! But Emily wasn't quick enough to grab the other two, and as she tried to reach them, the bear rolled back to where he'd been before. Two of the lockets were still trapped!

Philip looked serious. He held out his feather as though it was a magic wand. "Time for the armpits."

Emily didn't feel right about this at all. What if the grumpy bear woke up?

But they had no option. Philip reached up on tiptoe, leaning right over the bear to get to his armpit. The girls held their breath. The feather inched beneath the bear's furry arm and Philip began to tickle, grinning to himself and singing,

"Bear, oh bear!
Sleeping there,
Move your body a little bit
We're just going to tickle it."

Emily held out her hands, ready to snatch up the other two lockets the moment the bear moved. They'd nearly done it!

But then a yellow eye popped open. Then another.

"ROOOOAAAARRRRRRR!"

All of Philip's feathers were plastered back against his body as the bear roared a whole winter's stale breath over him.

Philip tumbled away across the cave floor. The bear shuffled up to sit, resting his giant paws on his knees.

The friends scrambled behind another rock, almost as big as the first one they'd hidden behind outside the cave. But this one wasn't quite large enough to hide them. Cranky the bear stared at them, as

though he thought they were responsible
for the most terrible crime.

"Why did you wake me up?" he
growled, gazing round at them through
bleary eyes. "I was having a lovely dream.
It was about fluffy clouds and sweets!"
His face fell. "I was just about to eat a
chewy caramel."

"We're very sorry, Cranky," Aisha said.

"Wicked Selena stole Sweetblossom's lockets and hid them with you," Emily said, pointing to the unicorn who trembled by the cave mouth. "We need them back so that spring can begin."

"Please," Aisha added. She crossed her fingers behind her back and hoped Cranky would understand.

He shuffled to his feet. It was like watching a mountain rise out of the ground, especially when he reached his arms above his head and let out a giant yawn. His stomach gave a noisy growl and they all realised that the bear was probably very hungry after his long sleep. No wonder he'd been dreaming about delicious things to eat.

He snatched up the lockets, dangling them in the air. "Are these what you want?" he growled, turning towards the rock.

"Yes, please!" Emily and Aisha said together. They held out their hands, but he strode past them – straight out of the cave.

"Well, you can't have them," he called back over a furry shoulder, pushing past Sweetblossom and out into the forest. "That's what you get for waking me up!"

The others ran to the cave entrance and watched Cranky walk away, his

huge body rolling from side to side. They sighed heavily.

"At least we have one locket," Aisha said faintly, holding out the one she'd managed to rescue.

Emily took the locket from her and walked over to Sweetblossom. "Here you are," she said, looping the locket around the unicorn's neck. She stood back to admire her work, and a tiny glow came from beneath the thick hair of the unicorn's blue mane.

All four of them looked up into the sky, shielding their eyes with their hands. From between the trees, they could see the golden orb of the sun slowly inch back towards the horizon – the day was getting longer before their eyes! It was changing from a short winter day to a longer, brighter spring day.

"This gives us more time to get the other two lockets," Emily realised.

They had to get the lockets back from Cranky or else there'd be no springtime in Enchanted Valley!

Story Two

✦✦✦★★✦★★✦★★✦✦✦

Midday Mayhem

Chapter One
Cranky the Climber

The friends stood in the forest, ready to chase after the remaining two lockets.

"Now, where has that bear gone?" asked Philip.

Suddenly, there was the sound of something crashing through the trees.

"That sounds like Cranky to me!"

exclaimed Emily.

Sweetblossom began to trot towards where the sounds were coming from and the others quickly followed.

It didn't take them long to find the bear. All they had to do was follow another trail – tree after tree had broken branches and some were leaning at an awkward angle.

In the distance they saw Cranky, standing on his hind legs, looking up into some branches.

"Here! Let's hide!" Aisha scrambled into a bush. Inside it, there was a space they could all fit in. One after the other, they stepped over the branches until they were hidden.

Emily pulled back a branch and they watched Cranky start climbing again.

"What is he trying to reach?" Philip asked.

Aisha looked up and pointed. "There, see! A bees' nest." They could just make out a small, round, brown object high in the branches.

Cranky heaved himself up on to a branch. He wobbled dangerously as the branch bent beneath his weight.

"I'm not sure he should be doing that," Philip said.

"I don't think the tree is sure, either," said Emily, as the groan of a creaking branch filled the air.

The bear gave a huge grunt as he tried to lift himself up on to another branch, and another. Soon, he was high above the ground. He reached a paw towards the bees' nest.

"He's hungry!" Sweetblossom said. "He wants the honey."

"Of course! He's been hibernating and hasn't eaten for months," Emily agreed. "He must be very hungry indeed."

Aisha poked her head further out of the bush to see. "Oh dear," she said, "it doesn't look very …"

Emily looked out, too – just in time to see Cranky shove his paw into the bees' nest. Parts of it fell away and crumbled to the ground. It looked as though it had been there all winter. No bees lived there now. He pulled away his paw and stared at it.

"No honey," said Aisha, shaking her head.

"Not a drop," agreed Emily.

Cranky gave a roar of despair and

slumped down on the branch. It trembled beneath him. Then there was a crack and a snap and the branch split in two, sending Cranky tumbling through the air. He plunged to the ground, where he landed in a pile of leaves and sat up to rub his head.

"I said he shouldn't do that," Philip commented, shaking his head.

"Poor Cranky," Sweetblossom said.

But Aisha and Emily were too busy grinning at each other to listen.

"Are you thinking what I'm thinking?" Aisha said.

"Yes," said Emily. "If we can find some honey, perhaps we can persuade Cranky to give us the lockets."

Chapter Two
Surly's Surprise

Philip began to dance around so that
his feathers floated in the air. "What a
plan!" he cried. "It's perfect!" He then
immediately slapped his paw over his
mouth as he realised what a noise he was
making.

Fortunately, Cranky had already

moved off towards another tree. He didn't notice the featherhog's excited outburst. Emily and Aisha followed Philip out and brushed the leaves and twigs off their onesies. Sweetblossom used her horn to hold aside the branches and stepped out neatly, shaking her mane.

"I know just the place," she said. "We can go to Surly's Sweet Shop! He uses honey in his sweets. He might have some left over."

"Hooray!" Emily and Aisha cried.

"And we can get you some springtime clothes on the way," Sweetblossom said.

She was right – the girls were already feeling very warm in their onesies!

Sweetblossom began to lead them out of the forest.

A butterfly with pink wings flapped

past them, looking sad. "Please, Sweetblossom, when will the flowers open? I'm very thirsty for a drink of nectar."

Sweetblossom lowered her head so the butterfly could take a rest on her horn. "I'm so sorry, Tilly. Without my Blossoming Buds locket, there is nothing I can do," Sweetblossom explained.

"But we've got a plan to get it back!" Philip told Tilly, bouncing with excitement.

"Oh, thank you," said Tilly, as she fluttered away again.

As they walked on, they saw more creatures waiting hopefully beside tightly closed buds. A hummingbird floated above some foxgloves and a little frog in a small pond licked a waterlily bud hopefully. Aisha and Emily tried not to feel too sad – they'd fix this for Enchanted Valley. They just had to!

After a while, there grew more space between the trees and before they knew it, they emerged on the other side of the forest. They were standing by a large, blue lake with fluffy ducks, all the colours of the rainbow. There was even a large bird, standing on one leg, that was as pink as a flamingo but wearing a black felt hat with red pom-poms dangling from the brim.

"What's that bird?" Emily asked.

"Ah!" Sweetblossom said. "That's a flaminco – a flamingo that likes to dance the flamenco." She stamped her little hooves against the ground. "*Olé!*"

Emily and Aisha shared a chuckle. Would Enchanted Valley ever stop surprising them?

"And he might have some clothes for you." Sweetblossom went to speak to the flaminco, who was only too happy to give the girls some springtime clothes: a buttercup-yellow skirt for Emily and a T-shirt with flowers on for Aisha.

"Thank you so much!" the girls said to him.

"*De nada,*" he replied with a long-necked bow.

Sweetblossom headed towards a little

hut on the edge of the lake. On one side, it had a serving hatch and a chalkboard menu. On the other side was a window filled with jars of sweets and a door that stood open. Bunting hung from the roof and brightly coloured balloons bobbed in the air.

They peered through the door. Behind the counter stood a troll with a tufty head. He was wearing a cotton apron and held a silver scoop full of green sweets. He was pouring the sweets into a jar labelled *Goblin Gummies*. Other jars lined the hut's shelves, full of sweets called Pixie Sticks, Melty Mallows and Valley Violets.

As Surly placed the jar back on the shelf, he spotted the friends.

"Come in, come in!" he said, beaming

at them and not looking surly at all. He
used to be a guard for Selena, but after
Emily and Aisha had helped Slumbertail
the sleep unicorn to defeat her, he'd had
a change of heart.

"How good to see you!" he cried. "Do sit down!" He dragged out some stools from behind the counter. "You can try my newest sweets." He held out a paper bag, twisted shut at the corners. "They're called Surly's Surprise. They look like lemon drops, but they taste of cherry."

"No, thank you," Emily said. She couldn't believe she was turning down a sweet. "We'd love to try your sweets, but we're in a big rush."

"Selena is up to her old tricks," Aisha added. "She's stolen Sweetblossom's lockets."

Sweetblossom nodded her head from where she stood in the doorway.

Surly's smile dropped from his face. "Not again! I know how bad she can be. How can I help?"

"Do you have any honey?" piped up Philip. "Like, a *lot* of honey?"

"Enough to feed a bear?" Sweetblossom added.

Surly shook his head. "I'm afraid not. I use honey to make my sweets, but I just used the last of it for my Surly's Surprises."

"Oh." Emily felt her hope start to die, but she couldn't give up now! "Where do you get your honey from?" she asked.

"The bees at Tumble Meadow," Surly said. "They make the sweetest honey in all of the kingdom!"

Sweetblossom's face lit up. "Of course!" She nuzzled her face up against Surly in thanks, then she turned to the girls with a smile. "Let's go!"

Chapter Three
Tumble Meadow

The friends ran out of the sweet shop,
calling their thanks to Surly as they went.

"This way!" Sweetblossom cried.

The sun was high in the sky by the
time they arrived at Tumble Meadow.
Long grasses danced in the breeze and
they could see all sorts of wildflowers in

bud, just waiting to burst open.

"We have to make spring come," said
Sweetblossom, bending to touch her nose
to a hairy poppy bud that dangled from
its stem like a tiny lantern. "This meadow
should be all the colours of the rainbow
by now."

"Don't worry," Aisha said, putting an
arm around the unicorn's neck. "The bees
will help us, I'm sure."

They made their
way to the centre of
the meadow and
found several
big straw hives.
Large, fluffy
bees buzzed
around
them.

Emily squinted. "Look how they're flying."

Aisha looked closer and gasped in delight. The big, fat bees were rolling over and over, doing somersaults through the air. It looked as though they were giddy with happiness!

"What strange bumblebees," Emily said, watching one of them roll past her nose.

"They're not bumblebees, they're *tumble*bees," Sweetblossom explained. "A bit like bumblebees, but more playful."

"It makes me think of my gymnastics class," Aisha said. "It's as though they're rolling over on invisible mats."

"Well, here's hoping their good mood will make them give us some honey," Philip said, his tail feathers quivering in excitement.

He hopped over to the nearest hive and stood up on his hind legs to politely knock a furry paw against the door. There was a buzzing sound that grew louder and a little cloud of tumblebees tumbled out of the door.

"Synchronised gymnastics!" Aisha cried. "This just gets better and better."

"Why, thank you." All the bees spoke exactly together, to make their buzzing voices loud enough for the girls to hear. "Would you like to see our bee pyramid? We've been practising for ages."

Aisha would have loved to see it – she thought it would be much better than a human pyramid. But she knew there was no time. She could feel the sun's warmth on the top of her head.

"I'm sorry," she said. "But we're in a big

rush. Do you have any spare honey?"

"It's for a cranky bear," Emily
explained.

The buzzing slowed down. "Oh dear,"
the bees said. "We can't give you honey
for a bear."

Philip hopped from foot to foot. "Why

not?" he cried. "It's very important."

"Bears always steal our honey," the bees buzzed. "Normally we'd help, but not if it's for a bear!"

From behind the girls, Sweetblossom stepped forward and the buzzing suddenly became very fast indeed.

"Sweetblossom!" the bees cried. "You're the unicorn who starts spring for us!"

She nodded her head. "For you, and for all the creatures – even grumpy bears," Sweetblossom said. "But this year, Selena has stolen my lockets. As you clever bees know, spring can't start without them." The bees dipped in the air, as though they'd suddenly run out of energy. "She gave the lockets to the bear. That's why we want some honey – to exchange for the lockets and let spring begin."

Sweetblossom looked up at the sky. "But we need to do this before the end of today."

"The spring babies won't be born if we don't," added Philip.

The tumblebees brightened up at that, and did some loop-the-loops through the air. "Why didn't you say? We do have one jar left," the bees said together. "We always save one for an emergency – and this is definitely an emergency."

"Exactly," said Sweetblossom, flicking her tail. "We're glad you understand."

"No spring means no flowers, and no flowers means no nectar, and no nectar means … NO HONEY!" the bees cried.

"We won't let that happen," Emily told them. "Thank you so much."

Aisha was so excited, she did a

cartwheel across the meadow. The bees buzzed and cheered their applause.

"You're as good as us!" they cried.

"Almost," Aisha said, brushing the grass off her trousers.

"Follow us to the last jar!" the tumblebees cried, setting off in a cloud of excited roly-polies.

The four friends shared a grin.

This honey would save the whole of Enchanted Valley!

Chapter Four
Sweet Acrobatics

The tumblebees bounced and rolled
through the air, out of the meadow and
towards a thick clump of brambles.

Aisha remembered the prickly brambles
in the forest and hoped these wouldn't be
as bad, but as they drew closer, she saw
they were even worse. The brambles were

a knot of branches and thorns.

"Oh no," Emily sighed. "Please tell me that's not where the honey is."

The tumblebees dived through a narrow space between two thick stems. "The jar is here!" they cried. "It's on a tree stump."

"Can you get it out for us?" Emily asked, hopefully.

The tumblebees zoomed back out. "Oh no. It's too heavy for us."

"Then how did you get it in there?" Philip asked.

"The queen bee magics it into a hiding place, but she's still asleep right now. Until spring arrives properly she can't help." The tumblebees tumbled down through the air as their spirits drooped.

"Oh, what a problem!"

"A very big problem," murmured Emily. She looked at Aisha. "Shall we try to get past the brambles?"

"Yes, definitely," Aisha said. "We've come too far to give up now."

"Why don't I try first?" Philip said. "I'm smaller than you two."

Sweetblossom helpfully reached out with her horn to hold back some of the brambles and trampled down others with her hooves. Philip turned himself sideways and tried to squeeze through the hole but …

"Ooh! Ow! Ah! Eeee!" He sprang back, rubbing his bottom. "Well, that wasn't very dignified."

"Oh, Philip! We're sorry you hurt yourself," Aisha cried.

As Aisha comforted Philip, Emily
looked at the brambles. Her mind was
working hard, trying to find a solution.
All she needed to do was inspect every
detail of the hedge.

"There!" she cried. She pointed to a
girl-sized gap just above their heads.
"And there's another one!" Deeper in
there was another large space between
the brambles, but it was much lower. She

peered through the needles and spotted a third gap. This one was the highest of them all!

"They're all just big enough for us to get through," Aisha pointed out, "but how do we reach them?" As she said this, a tumblebee tumbled past her nose. She watched it and her face lit up. She snapped her fingers. "Gymnastics!" she cried.

"YES!" cried the tumblebees in a chorus of excitement. "You can leap through the gaps in the brambles."

"Exactly!" said Emily. "I think we'll both have to go in, because one of us will need to give the other one a boost to get through that last gap."

Aisha grinned at Emily. "Let's do it! Come on, I'll show you some moves."

They went to stand on a clear patch of grass and the tumblebees and Aisha showed Emily how to take a running leap – though it was a flying leap for the tumblebees. Then they talked Emily through the perfect dive roll – a running jump combined with a forward roll. All the time, the sun grew higher in the sky.

Emily wiped the sweat from her brow. "OK, I think I'm ready."

The two of them arranged themselves at a short distance from the brambles.

"Good luck!" cried Sweetblossom. She pawed the ground nervously.

"Tally-ho!" called Philip, doing his best to give them a thumbs up – though it was difficult without any actual thumbs.

The tumblebees counted them in. "One, two, three!"

Aisha set off first. She ran towards the first gap – the one higher than their heads. After gaining speed, she took off into the air, using a fallen log as a springboard. She pointed her arms ahead of her and neatly dived through the gap, landing in a perfect forward roll. She sprang up and out of the way, just as Emily followed her in. Yes, they'd done it!

Next, they had to clamber through the gap that was down by the ground. They flattened themselves and wriggled beneath the branches. They had to be very flexible and get into all sorts of positions to make their way through. Aisha's T-shirt caught on a thorn, but she managed to free herself. They climbed to their feet and Aisha blew a lock of hair out of her face.

"Nearly there!" she told Emily, who nodded. She looked determined to pull this off!

The last gap would be the hardest. It was up high. Emily linked her fingers and bent over. "Use my hand as a step," she said. "Then leap as high as you can!"

Aisha placed her foot in Emily's linked hands. She bounced up and down on her other knee, storing up energy. "Count me in," she told Emily.

"One, two, THREE!" Emily cried.

Aisha leapt into the air and performed the most perfect dive roll through the gap. Emily heard her land with a soft *thwump* on the other side, amongst

the leaves and twigs. There was a scrambling sound and then Aisha cried, "I've found it! I've found the jar of honey!"

She used the tree stump to launch herself into another dive roll back to Emily. She held out the jar. The honey was the exact colour of buttercups mixed with sunshine. It was definitely worth all the effort to get to it.

The two of them performed all their acrobatics in reverse, arriving back outside the bramble hedge.

"Well done! Well done!" cried the tumblebees. "We wish we had a gold medal to give you."

Emily and Aisha didn't need medals. They just needed to see spring return to Enchanted Valley. And now they had just what they needed to make that happen!

Chapter Five
A Fair Swap

The tumblebees led the girls to a baker's shop near the meadow. It was built into the side of a hill and there was a little stone oven where loaves were baked on top of hot bricks. A dragon fly – a small dragon with insect wings – floated in the air, wearing a tiny white chef's hat and

a crisp apron, as he drew fresh loaves out
on a wooden paddle.

Aisha was still carrying her jar of
honey, and placed it down on the grass.

"Are you looking for some fresh bread
to go with that?" the dragon fly buzzed.
He slid a loaf off his wooden paddle.
"Here, this is perfect with honey!"

"Oh, thank you!" the girls chorused. They borrowed a knife from the dragon fly baker and cut the bread into slices, then smeared them with the honey. Then they wrapped the honey sandwiches up in greaseproof paper.

"Good luck!" the baker called after them, as they set off. The tumblebees flew with the friends back to the forest.

They found Cranky climbing another tree.

"Whoa! Whoa! Grrrrrrr!" His arms flapped, his body flipped, and the bear fell back through the branches and landed with a crash on the ground.

As he climbed to his feet, the girls stepped between the trees and held out the honey sandwiches.

"Hello, Cranky," Emily said. "We've

brought you something."

"Honey sandwiches," Aisha added.

Cranky's eyes lit up. "For me?" He pointed a giant paw at his chest.

"Yes," Aisha said, "if you give us the lockets." She could see them glinting at the base of the tree, where Cranky had left them.

The bear froze. He started to shake his head. "Oh no," he said. "There's something I want more than food." His tummy gave a loud growl, as though it didn't agree.

"Are you sure?" Emily said.

The bear shook his head again. "I don't want your honey."

Cranky's stomach growled noisily again, giving him away. He folded his paws tightly over his tummy, as though that would stop it.

Emily winked at Aisha. Aisha gave a small smile of understanding.

"That's a shame," Emily said in a loud voice. "We'll just leave the sandwiches here, then."

Aisha made a great show of placing the

sandwiches down on a tree stump. Then the two of them started to walk away.

"What are you doing?" Philip asked.

"You'll see," whispered Emily.

They all went to hide behind a bush and peeked out from behind the branches. Sure enough, once Cranky thought they'd gone, he padded over to the tree stump and unwrapped the sandwiches, eating them noisily.

"Now!" whispered Emily. Aisha darted out and ran to the tree, snatching up a locket. But Cranky spotted what she was doing and gave a roar of disapproval. She began to run fast, out of his way – but not fast enough! Cranky swiped with his claws and she had to leap into a neat forward roll to escape him. He gave another giant roar.

"I only managed to get one," Aisha said, panting. She showed them the locket with the tiny cherry blossom inside: the Blossoming Buds locket. She looked back over her shoulder at the angry bear. "Should I try to get the other one?"

"Not now," Emily said. "He needs to calm down."

But it was too late for that. Cranky had spotted them and was stomping over.

"Quick! Climb on my back!" said

Sweetblossom. The girls scrambled up and pulled Philip up to sit between them. Then the unicorn launched herself into the air.

They flew all the way back to Tumble Meadow, where the girls slid back down to the ground. Aisha placed the locket around Sweetblossom's neck. Immediately, the whole meadow burst into flower, creased petals unfurling and raising their heads to the sun. They were surrounded by reds and purples, pinks and yellows.

The tumblebees cheered and tumbled in a circle around the girls in a dance to say thank you. Then they busily buzzed away to start collecting nectar again.

The girls smiled at one another. Soon, there would be enough honey for the whole valley. There was just one of

Sweetblossom's lockets left to retrieve —
and they had to get it back so that Philip
could meet his baby brother.

Story Three

✦ ⭑ ★ ⭑ ✦ ⭑ ★ ⭑ ✦

Spring Baby Sunset

Chapter One
Baby Flowers

The sun was starting to dip to the west. The friends had achieved so much, but if they didn't get that last locket back Philip's baby brother – and all the spring babies in the kingdom – wouldn't be born.

"Cranky said he wanted something

more than food," Aisha said, tapping a finger against her lips. "What do you think it could be?"

"If we can find it for him, maybe we can exchange it for the last locket," Emily said. "Come on, let's go and see if we can get him to tell us."

They started to walk back towards the forest, leaving Tumble Meadow behind. The spring flowers were so pretty now they were open! But as they entered

another field, the flowers changed.

"None of them are open," Aisha said, looking around. She was right – the flowers were all tightly furled, still waiting to blossom. But their buds were much bigger than any of the other flowers in Enchanted Valley.

"I don't understand," said Emily. "Sweetblossom, you have the Blossoming Buds locket back – so why aren't these flowers showing their petals?"

"Ah," said Sweetblossom. "Well, you see, the spring babies of Enchanted Valley are extra special. They are born differently to other babies and this is where it happens."

The girls looked around the meadow, wondering what she meant. Then one of the buds gave a wriggle.

Emily's eyes lit up with excitement. "I think I understand!" she cried. She pointed at another flower bud. The tightly furled petals moved and shifted with what looked like the shape of … a tiny foot! "Each flower bud contains a baby!" She looked at Sweetblossom. "Is that right?"

The unicorn smiled and dipped her head. "When the flowers open, the baby animals are born." Then her smile faded. "But without the magic of the third locket, that can't happen."

"Mum! Dad!" Philip cried, and darted
across the field towards two larger
featherhogs. They must have been his
parents! They were standing beside a
flower head that waved and bobbed in
the breeze, as light as a feather. They
were holding each other's paws and
watching the flower closely.

"Philip!" His dad scooped him up into a hug and his mother bent to stroke his cheek.

"Is this …" Philip stared at the flower head. "Is this my baby brother?" His eyes were wide with longing. The girls could see how much it meant to him to have a new member of the family.

"I wonder if he's dreaming in there," Philip said, gently tapping a paw against the flower bud. "Knock, knock, baby brother! Are you dreaming of being a featherhog?"

"That's it!" Emily cried. She hugged Philip so tight that his feathers tickled her nose.

"What did I say?" he asked, looking from her face to Aisha's.

Emily was grinning. "Cranky had a

dream, remember? We
woke him up from it."

"That's right," said
Aisha. "He said it
was a lovely
dream. Maybe
we could
help him
fall asleep
again so he
could carry
on dreaming?"

"You can't choose to go back to
the same dream though, can you?"
Sweetblossom asked.

"No," Emily admitted. "And he only
just woke up from hibernation. I don't
think we can send him back to that kind
of deep sleep. But what if we could make

his dream come true in real life?"

Aisha's face lit up with understanding. "Yes! He said he was having a lovely dream. Something about clouds and sweets … Maybe if we could create that dream, he'd be happy enough to give us the locket."

Chapter Two
Sky Shapes

They found the bear in the same clearing where they'd left the honey sandwiches. Cranky was lying on his back, using a patch of moss as a pillow. He had his legs crossed and the last locket dangled from one claw. He gazed up at the clouds, trying to count them – almost as though he was counting sheep.

"That one looks like a duck!" they heard him say to himself. "And that one looks like a featherhog." He wriggled on his back.

"Oh goodness," Aisha said, "I hope he doesn't mind if we disturb him again."

"What choice do we have?" said Emily.

Another cloud passed over the sun, low in the sky. "We hardly have any time left!"

They crossed the forest floor, trying not to make too much noise.

"Excuse me, Cranky," Emily said, using her most polite voice. "Do you mind if we ask you a question?"

He grunted and heaved himself up to sitting. He grabbed the locket from his foot. "You two, again! What do you want this time?" He looked at their hands, clearly hoping for more honey sandwiches.

"When we woke you up—" Aisha began.

"Don't remind me," Cranky interrupted.

Aisha cleared her throat and tried again. "When we woke you up, what were you dreaming of?"

A big grin spread across Cranky's furry face. "Oh, it was the best dream! Real life could never be as brilliant as that dream."

"What if it could be?" Emily said.

He frowned. "What do you mean?"

Aisha took a step closer. "If we promised to make your dream come true, would you give us the last locket?"

Cranky threw his head back and laughed. "I was flying on a fluffy white cloud. Sweets were raining down over me." He suddenly stopped laughing. "If you can make that dream come true, you have definitely earned the locket."

"It's a deal!" Aisha reached out a hand to shake on it, but then changed her mind. Cranky had *very* big claws.

She went back to Emily. "Did you hear that?" she asked.

Emily nodded, her face pale. "Well done on getting him to promise." She gulped. "But how are we going to recreate a dream like that?"

They went to tell Philip and Sweetblossom about Cranky's dream.

"First stop, the sweet shop!" Philip said, clapping his paws together. "Follow me!"

He marched out of the forest and they followed in a line.

Surly was still behind his counter. He was arranging the jars of sweets according

to colour, making them into a rainbow along his shelves.

"Surly, please can we have some sweets?" Aisha asked.

"A *lot* of sweets," Emily added. "It's to help save the valley!"

Surly grinned at them. "Of course!" He turned to the shelves. "Now, which are my absolute best sweets?" He reached up on tiptoe for a jar with a special gold lid, and another jar with a silver lid. Then he slid them across the counter to the girls. "These are my honey dropsicles."

Honey dropsicles? The girls smiled at each other. That couldn't be more perfect for a bear!

Chapter Three
A Dream Come True

"Oh, thank you, Surly!" Aisha cried. She took one jar, and Emily took another.

"They're not for us," Emily explained. She could never eat this many sweets!

"What are they for, then?" Surly asked.

The girls explained how they wanted to make Cranky's dream come true. Surly took off his apron and came out from behind the counter.

"I'm coming to help," he announced, and everyone cheered. It was so great to have friends who would pitch in.

They stepped outside and Surly turned the sign round so that it read: *Back Soon*.

"Right!" He clapped his hands together. "What next?"

"Next, we need a cloud," Aisha said, biting her lip.

"Or something that looks like a cloud," Emily pointed out, her eyes shining.

"Fluffy, the cloud puppy!" they cried together. He was another friend they felt certain would help.

Sweetblossom flew up into the sky to call to him. "Oh, Fluffy!"

A large cloud began to move across

the sky, heading straight towards Surly's Sweet Shop.

"Do you think it's Fluffy?" Aisha asked. "That was quick!"

Sweetblossom came down to land beside them. "I think so. He must like you very much!"

Fluffy landed on the grass and gave a small yip of excitement. The girls ran to throw their arms around his neck. They buried their faces in his white, fluffy fur. It was just like cuddling a gigantic ball of cotton wool!

Pulling back, they explained all about Cranky and the locket. "Would you let him ride you, as a dream come true?" Aisha asked, when they got to the end of their story.

"Of course!" Fluffy barked. "Anything

for you. Come on, climb up!"

Aisha bent down and scooped Philip up in her arms. Then she and Emily scrambled up on to Fluffy's back. It was so soft and cosy! With a joyous bark, he sprang into the air. Just like that, they were flying! Sweetblossom floated beside them. The forest below looked like it was made of miniature trees. Thank goodness

they had Fluffy to get them there quickly!

They came down to land in the clearing and Cranky's eyes grew wide.

"You're riding a cloud!" he cried.

"Come and join us!" Emily called, beckoning him.

Cranky lumbered over and heaved himself on to Fluffy's back behind the two girls. His paws reached round Emily's waist to hang on. His brown fur was almost as soft as Fluffy's.

Aisha bent down to whisper in Fluffy's ear. "Are you OK to carry us all?"

"You bet – watch this!" He took a running leap into the sky – just like Aisha's gymnastics – and they circled round and round in the air. Every now and then, they'd bump up against another cloud and it would bob merrily out of the way.

Meanwhile, Surly had climbed on to Sweetblossom's back, clutching the jars of sweets. He tossed handful after handful into the air, as Sweetblossom soared above them, until sweets rained through the sky!

Cranky gave a big whoop of delight. Emily could feel it vibrating against her back.

"You made my dream come true!" he cried. "You really did it!" He reached to snatch a honey dropsicle out of the air, and popped it into his mouth. "I'm so happy!" he said, between chews.

They came back down to land and slid off Fluffy's back. Cranky pulled out the locket and handed it over into Aisha's

open palm. "This is yours now," he said.
"I'm sorry I was a grumpy, cranky
bear. I'm so glad you woke me up after
all. Thank you."

Chapter Four
Sweet Enough

The sun dipped towards the horizon and
the sky started to merge into all sorts of
colours – red and gold, pink and violet.
It looked almost as pretty as the dawn
sky back at Queen Aurora's castle, but
the girls knew there wasn't any time
to waste. They had to fasten the locket

around Sweetblossom's neck, where it belonged! They rushed over and reached around her soft, furry neck to fasten the chain with a click. Their unicorn friend had all her lockets now!

But suddenly there was a flash of blue lightning and a rumble of thunder. Selena landed beside them, her sharp horn piercing the air.

"What are you doing?" she cried. "I left my lockets with an angry bear, and now look at him!" She shook her mane in disgust. "He's gone all soppy and soft."

Sweetblossom politely cleared her throat. "Whose lockets, Selena?"

The evil unicorn's nostrils flared. "Mine!" She trotted over to Sweetblossom and bared her teeth, ready to snatch them back again.

"Oh no, you don't!" Aisha grabbed
some crusts of honey sandwiches that
Cranky had left on a tree stump. She
threw them straight at Selena and the
drips of honey spattered her mane.

She shook her head angrily. "Argh! My
beautiful mane! Get it out!" She tried
to rub herself against a tree trunk to get
clean, but that only pushed the honey
deeper into her hair.

There was a buzzing noise and suddenly a cloud of tumblebees burst into the clearing. They circled around Selena, attracted by the honey.

"Get away from me!" she cried, trying to shake them off.

"Yay, honey!" cried the tumblebees as they tumbled towards her. She suddenly bolted and the tumblebees chased after her, drawing circles through the air as they laughed and called out. Selena raced faster and faster, glancing back over her shoulder until – *oof!* – she ran straight into Cranky.

His eyes narrowed. His lips curled back from his teeth. Then he let out a huge roar that sent Selena's mane flying all over her face. She blew a sticky strand out of her eyes and looked up at Cranky, her flanks trembling.

"What did you say about being soppy and soft?" Cranky asked. Before she could answer him, he let out another loud roar. Selena whimpered, then ran away as fast as her hooves would carry her, swerving wildly between the trees.

"And don't come back!" Cranky called after her.

Everyone gathered in the clearing. Aisha and Emily licked the honey from their fingers. Finally, the three lockets were safely back with Sweetblossom. The crowd of friends cheered and waved their arms in the air, hugging each other and dancing round in circles.

"Hooray for Emily and Aisha!" they cried. "Hooray for Philip!"

Then they all caught sight of the look in Philip's eyes and fell silent to hear him speak.

"I think," said Philip, as he looked around at the flowers, "that I'd like to meet my brother now."

Chapter Five
A Poppy's Gift

They all went with Philip to the field of flowers. The buds had all started to wriggle!

"It's time!" Philip cried. A moment later the flowers began to gently open and unfurl to reveal their surprises. And what surprises they were! A pair of rabbits peered into a cluster of primroses to see a tiny bunny arrive in the world. Close by them, a mother duck watched a row of fluffy ducklings waddle out of the purple bells of a foxglove and drop to the ground around her webbed feet.

"It's all so sweet!" Aisha said, looking from flower to flower as they made their way over to Philip's parents. The air was full of cries of delight and little noises of

welcome. Sweetblossom looked as though she was glowing with pride.

"It's all been worth it," she said. The girls couldn't agree more.

"Mum! Dad!" Philip rushed over to his parents and they drew him close, just as a poppy began to unfurl its papery red petals. Aisha and Emily leaned over to see – they didn't want to miss this for anything!

Right at the heart of the flower, a tiny creature was curled up. Its little eyes were firmly shut, but then the breeze ruffled its downy feathers and it slowly woke. The baby featherhog climbed to its tiny feet, balancing on a petal. Philip's mum reached a paw into the poppy so that he could climb out. She held the little one to her chest and planted a kiss on his head.

"We'll call him Freddy," Philip's dad announced, wiping away a tear.

Their mum pulled a blanket off her shoulder and wrapped it around the tiny one's body to stop it from shivering in the breeze. It must have been a surprise for Freddy to suddenly have no petals wrapped around him after all this time!

The baby featherhog gazed up at his big brother, letting out a mewl of greeting.

"Hello, little one," Philip said. His smile

faded as he looked at the blanket. "Oh, I'm sorry, I didn't have time to get you a present."

Suddenly, a large paw reached over everyone's heads. From it dangled a cuddly teddy bear. "Freddy can have this," said Cranky. "He needs it more than me."

"Oh, thank you!" Philip took the cuddly toy from him and held it out to his brother. The little one immediately reached out his front paws and took the teddy bear, snuggling into it for comfort.

Philip looked up at Cranky. "I'll make you a pillow with my feathers, once they've grown back." It was true, they were looking a bit thin after all their adventures. "Then you won't have to use moss as a pillow any more."

Cranky hugged himself with happiness.

"Thank you!" he growled. "That will be just perfect."

"That was very good of you," Aisha whispered up to Cranky. "If you carry on like that, we might have to rename you 'Cuddly'!"

"Steady on," Cranky chuckled.

"Now!" said Sweetblossom. "The Spring Beginnings Festival can start!"

It was as though the whole of Enchanted Valley heard her. Creatures flooded out from everywhere! Sweetblossom twirled her horn and a spiral of sparkles floated out on the air, to settle in the shape of … a maypole! Philip rushed to grab a ribbon and spin and twirl and thread around the others. Gnomes were weaving flower garlands and Chef Yummytum handed out thick

slices of yellow buttercup cake.

Queen Aurora walked over to the girls. "Thank you so much," she said. "You brought spring to Enchanted Valley."

"It's so pretty!" Emily said.

"I'm so glad we got to meet the babies," Aisha added.

As the sun finally dipped beyond the horizon, the tumblebees crowded around Aisha and Emily.

"Let us show you our acrobatics!" they cried.

As the two girls watched, the tumblebees circled and flipped, flying up and down in the air, their tiny wings a blur of activity in the colourful sunset. The bees gathered in a chain around them, and made waves through the air until they flew off in a long line towards another set of friends.

"I think it's time for us to go home," Aisha said, and Emily nodded.

The flaminco came back with the girls' onesies and they thanked him for lending them the clothes before changing back into them.

"*De nada!*" he said, with a flourish.

"Goodbye, girls," said Queen Aurora.

"And thank you again!" Sweetblossom called.

"Before you go," said Aurora, "I'd like to give you something." She handed over two little charms in the shape of teddy bears. They looked a lot like Cranky,

only with a sleepy smile. "Thank you so much for saving the valley again."

The girls proudly put the charms on their keyrings, next to the others.

"Goodbye, Freddy and Philip!" Aisha cried, waving over to the family of featherhogs. Philip looked over, and waved a paw. His feathers fluttered in the 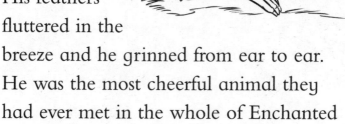 breeze and he grinned from ear to ear. He was the most cheerful animal they had ever met in the whole of Enchanted

Valley, and he was even happier now!

As they waved goodbye, their feet lifted up from the grass and they felt themselves floating into the air. Before they knew it, they settled back down in their tent.

The girls grinned at each other. "What an adventure!" said Aisha.

"Come on, girls!" Emily's dad called. "You'll miss the sunrise!"

The friends rushed out to Emily's parents. Their hot chocolates were still waiting for them, and they took a quick sip each.

They gasped as the sun came winking out beyond the furthest hedge, filling the world with light. The sky lit up in a hundred shades of pink and orange, red and purple. It reminded the girls of something – or some*one* – but neither of them mentioned it; they just sat in silence and soaked up the beautiful view.

Spring would be in full bloom soon, and the two friends couldn't wait!

The End

Join Emily and Aisha
for another adventure in...
Rosymane and
the Rescue Crystal

Emily and Aisha walked along the top
of the crumbling brick wall outside the
house where Aisha lived – Enchanted
Cottage. Treading carefully, they held
their arms out for balance.

"This is great practice for gymnastics,"
said Aisha, thinking of her favourite
sport.

The sun was shining through the trees,
and Emily spotted a perfect cluster of
ripe cherries right above her. "Don't
they look delicious?" she said to Aisha,

pointing up.

"Ooh, can you reach them?" Aisha asked.

Emily reached up as high as she could. "Whoa – whoooaaaa – OH!"

In a tumble, she fell on to the lawn, rolling in the grass.

"Are you all right?" Aisha called, leaping down beside her friend to reach out a hand. Emily grasped her fingers and pulled herself up to standing, brushing the grass off her blue trousers.

"I'm fine!" Honestly, Emily wasn't too bothered – she didn't think she'd hurt herself at all.

"No, look, you're injured," Aisha pointed at Emily's elbow.

Emily looked down and sure enough, a bright red scrape had appeared.

"Maybe I should get you a plaster," said Aisha.

But as she turned to go into the house, Emily cried out. "Aisha!"

"What is it?" Aisha asked. "Does it hurt?"

"No, it's not that. Look, my pocket is glowing." Emily reached into her trouser pocket and pulled out a glowing crystal keyring shaped like a unicorn.

Aisha dug out her identical keyring from her shorts. It was glowing too. "Oh, wow!" she gasped. "It must be Queen Aurora, calling us back to Enchanted Valley!"

The girls shared a smile. Enchanted Valley was a special secret they shared. It was a wonderful place where unicorns, pixies, dragons and all sorts of other magical creatures lived. The girls held the keyrings together so that the horns touched and immediately, coloured sparkles exploded all around them and they were lifted into the air.

A moment later, their feet came down to rest on soft grass and the sparkles disappeared around them like a melting cloud. A castle with twisty golden turrets like unicorn horns sat in the distance – Queen Aurora's home.

The girls felt a thrill of excitement. They were back in Enchanted Valley!

A tiny figure trotted out from beneath one of the golden turrets and clip-clopped across a drawbridge – it was Queen Aurora herself, come to welcome them! Her coat shone with all the colours of a sunrise – pink and purple, orange and red. The queen dipped her horn in a familiar greeting.

"Oh, thank you both for coming!" she cried. "It's so good to see you."

"How can we help?" Emily asked.

"Well, we have a visitor arriving soon," Queen Aurora explained.

"It's not Selena, is it?" Aisha said, panicking. Selena was a horrible unicorn who wanted to steal Aurora's crown and rule Enchanted Valley herself.

Fortunately, Emily and Aisha had been able to help Queen Aurora protect her kingdom.

Queen Aurora gave a gentle tinkle of laughter. "No, not Selena," she said. "It's the Crystal King. A unicorn who rules Crystal Valley, the kingdom next to ours. He's coming to see us!"

"A Crystal King!" Emily gasped. This was a whole new surprise. "What is HIS home like?"

Queen Aurora smiled. "You would love to see it — and maybe one day you will. Though it's next to Enchanted Valley it takes a long time to get there. There are beautiful crystals, sparkling as far as the eye can see, and the kindest creatures…"

She dipped her head. "I think you'd fit in well there."

Aisha couldn't wait to meet their new friend. "That sounds wonderful – will he bring some crystals with him?"

Queen Aurora laughed again. "Maybe! I'm glad you're excited. Even if you can't go to Crystal Valley now, I knew you'd want to be here to meet him."

The girls wouldn't have missed this for the world! But then Aisha saw Emily wince slightly as she bent her scraped elbow.

"Oh, Queen Aurora, can you help us? Emily hurt her elbow." Aisha pointed at the injury, even though Emily tried to hide it by covering her elbow with the other hand.

"It's nothing!" Emily said cheerily, but Aisha could tell her friend was in pain.

"Oh, you should have said so," the queen said. "Of course I can help. Come on!" She waved her horn over a shoulder. "Climb up!"

The girls scrambled on to her back, Aisha helping Emily. Then Queen Aurora rose into the air, cutting a path across fluffy white clouds. They travelled over Enchanted Valley, the sun lighting their way, and came to land on a tumbling hillside covered in a patchwork of fields. A stream snaked between the fields like a length of blue ribbon. Each field was a different colour, from pink to buttery yellow, violet to the deepest blue. It reminded Aisha of the quilt on her grandma's bed, only this was a real, living colourful blanket!

As the girls looked closer, they could see that the fields were ... *bouncy?* In each field, creatures tumbled and leapt, turning somersaults in the air, giggling with delight as they rose and fell, rose and fell. Their voices carried over to the girls.

"Wheeeee!"

"Boing!"

"The fields are like giant trampolines," Aisha gasped, gazing around. Just as she spoke, a little featherhog turned a dramatic loop-the-loop through the air, tail feathers flying.

"That's right." Queen Aurora smiled as a sleep pixie zoomed through the air, diving into a purple field, only to spring right back up again and shoot past their noses. "Welcome to Pillow Plains!"

Aisha couldn't see any plasters anywhere. "It looks super fun," she said. "But how will this help Emily's hurt elbow?"

"Ah, well, I need to introduce you to someone." Queen Aurora nodded over to a corner of a field and a figure separated from the others, trotting over to greet them. It was a unicorn, with a pale pink body that deepened to a bolder pink across her mane and tail.

"This is Rosymane. She is one of the Healing Crystal Unicorns," the queen told them.

"We're very pleased to meet you," said the girls, and Rosymane dipped her nose in greeting – it looked as soft and velvety as a marshmallow! Aisha could see a little pink crystal nestled inside a gold locket around her throat.

The unicorn blinked as she spotted the scrape on Emily's elbow. "I have just the thing for that!" As she reached round for her backpack, slung between her shoulders, Queen Aurora explained to the girls.

"Rosymane heals cuts and bruises. That's why she lives here at Pillow Plains."

"Ouch!" A sudden cry came from the corner of a yellow field as a tiny vampster tumbled into the gate, rubbing his leg as his wings fluttered above his shoulder blades. He was a hamster, with tiny vampire wings and little fangs poking out of the corners of his mouth.

"As you can see, quite a few bumps happen here," said Rosymane.

Rosymane daintily held a pink crystal between her teeth. She carefully lowered her head to touch the crystal to Emily's hurt elbow – *Whoosh!* A little cloud of sparkles appeared and then faded away to reveal that the scrape had gone … to be replaced with shiny, pink skin. Emily rubbed her elbow.

"That's amazing!" She looked down at the skin that moments ago had had a scrape. There was no scab or scar or anything! "How did you do that?" Emily always wanted to know the science behind things.

Rosymane smiled modestly. "It's the magic of the lockets," she said.

"Her special talent," added the queen, looking at Rosymane fondly.

The vampster came running over. Rosymane touched her crystal to his knee and he scampered off, throwing himself into a forward roll. "Vank you, Rosymane!" he called back.

A shape appeared on the horizon, and then another and another.

"It's the other Healing Crystal Unicorns!" Queen Aurora said. "I asked them to come here, so we could all meet the Crystal King together."

Read
Rosymane and the Rescue Crystal
to find out what adventures are in store for Aisha and Emily!

Also available

Book One:

Book Two:

Book Three:

Book Four:

Book Five: **Book Six:**

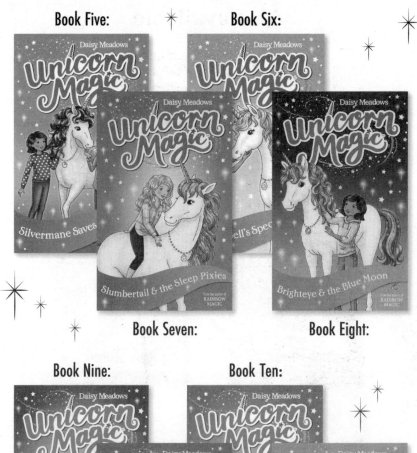

Book Seven: **Book Eight:**

Book Nine: **Book Ten:**

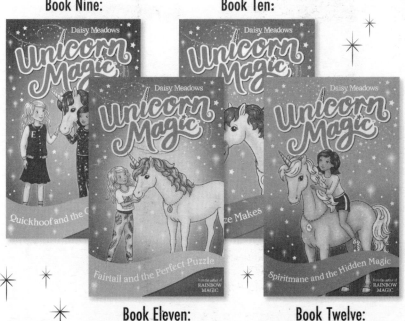

Book Eleven: **Book Twelve:**

Book Thirteen:

Rosymane and the Rescue Crystal

Book Fourteen:

Firebright and the Magic Medicine

Book Fifteen:

Twinkleshade and the Calming Charm

Book Sixteen:

Ripplestripe and the Peace Locket

Special One:

Snowstar and the Big Freeze

Special Two:

Sparklebeam's Holiday Adventure

Special Three:

Queen Aurora's Birthday Surprise